To Mom and Dad, who assure me I was a very truthful child.
It WAS the dog next door pulling up carrots from the garden,
NOT me. —M.B.

For Mom and Alejandro, with love —P.E.

A Note About Pangolins

The hero of this story is an animal not often featured in picture books.
Pangolins may look like reptiles, but they are actually scaly mammals that
live in the forests and grasslands of Africa and Asia. They are part of the
anteater family and are one of the world's most endangered species.

If you'd like to learn more about how you can help pangolins, check out
the work being done by the good people at pangolincrisisfund.org.

Text copyright © 2022 by Melinda Beatty
Jacket art and interior illustrations copyright © 2022 by Paola Escobar

All rights reserved. Published in the United States by Anne Schwartz Books, an imprint of Random House Children's
Books, a division of Penguin Random House LLC, New York.
Anne Schwartz Books and the colophon are trademarks of Penguin Random House LLC.

Visit us on the Web! rhcbooks.com
Educators and librarians, for a variety of teaching tools,
visit us at RHTeachersLibrarians.com

Library of Congress Cataloging-in-Publication Data is available upon request.
ISBN 978-0-593-18013-6 (trade) — ISBN 978-0-593-18014-3 (lib. bdg.) — ISBN 978-0-593-18015-0 (ebook)

The text of this book is set in 16-point Bailey Sans.
The illustrations were rendered digitally.
Book design by Sarah Hokanson

MANUFACTURED IN CHINA
10 9 8 7 6 5 4 3 2 1 First Edition

Melinda Beatty & Paola Escobar

Tell the Truth, PANGOLIN

a·s·b

anne schwartz books

Pangolin was enjoying himself
on the royal swing in the bright
summer sunshine, when . . .

"Ow!"

Pangolin got up and dusted himself off. "Heavens!
What have I done? And what will I tell the Queen?"

He hurried to the stables to ask his friend Badger.

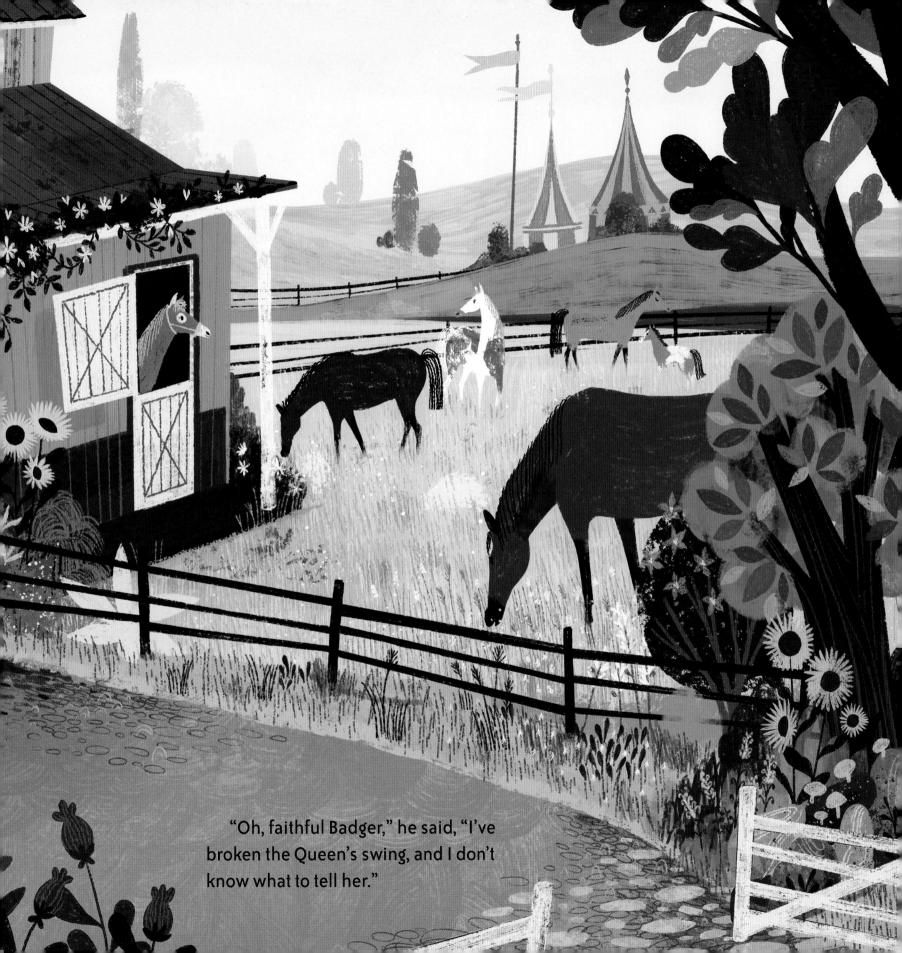

"Oh, faithful Badger," he said, "I've broken the Queen's swing, and I don't know what to tell her."

Badger scratched his stripy chin. "Maybe you can say that one of her musicians needed two new strings for his lute."

Pangolin thought about that.

"Thank you for your help, kind sir," he replied. "Maybe."

But Pangolin worried. So he went to the jousting field to ask his friend Goose.

"Oh, gallant Goose," he said, "I've broken the Queen's swing, and I don't know what to tell her."

Goose ruffled her downy feathers. "Perhaps you can say that a giant bird mistook the ropes for worms."

Pangolin thought about that.

"Thank you for your help, good mistress," he replied. "Perhaps."

But Pangolin *still* worried. So he went to
the castle gate to ask his friend Fox.
"Oh, noble Fox," he said, "I've broken
the Queen's swing, and I don't know what
to tell her."

Fox twitched his tall ears. "Might you say that the King needed to repair his royal jump rope?"

Pangolin thought about that.

"Thank you for your help, kind sir," he replied. "I might."

But Pangolin worried even *more*. So he went
to the kitchens to talk to his friend Cat.

"Oh, busy Cat," he said, "I've broken the
Queen's swing, and I don't know what to tell her."

Cat stroked her long whiskers. "You could say
a bear had something stuck between his teeth."

Pangolin thought about that.

"Thank you for your help, good mistress," he replied. "I could."

Now Pangolin worried more than he ever had before.
At the entrance to the Queen's chamber, he met his friend Pug.
"Oh, wise Pug," he said, "I've broken the Queen's swing, and
I don't know what to tell her."

Pug stuck out his tongue, crossed his eyes, and stood on his head. "Tell her it was abducted by aliens!"

Pangolin thought about that . . . but not very hard.

"Um, thank you for your help, kind sir," said Pangolin. And he got in line to see the Queen.

As he waited, Pangolin wondered if *anyone* had ever been so worried about *anything*.

When it was finally his turn, his feet felt heavy. His heart felt poundy. His stomach felt spinny and his knees felt knocky.

"G-g-g-good morning, Your Majesty," he said, bowing.
"Oh, Pangolin," wailed the Queen, "someone's broken my swing!"
Pangolin hung his head. "I know," he said miserably. "I was there."
"Well then, however did it happen?" she asked.

Pangolin swallowed hard.
"Um, a giant bird had something stuck
between his teeth!"
Pangolin's heart pounded faster.

"No, I mean, a lute-playing bear mistook it for a worm!"
Pangolin's stomach spun faster.

"Actually . . . *jump-roping aliens made off with the King?*"
Pangolin's knees knocked harder.
Finally . . .

The Queen bent down to look at him. "Pangolin, what's the matter?" she asked gently.

"Your Majesty," he whispered, "it wasn't a giant bird. Or a bear. Or aliens."

The Queen nodded.
"Well then, who was it?"
she asked.

Pangolin took a deep breath. "It was me, Your Majesty.
I broke the swing. And I'm very sorry."

The Queen kissed Pangolin on his scaly head. "Thank you for telling me, dear friend. Will you help me fix it?"
Pangolin smiled. "I will."